Oodles of Noodles

Written by Clare Helen Welsh

Illustrated by Sarah DeMonteverde

Collins

Hello! My name is Achara. Are you ready to start the tour?

We're travelling along a system of canals that have been turned into a giant market. It's a feast for the senses!

There are lots of sellers weighing fruit and vegetables.
This lady has a huge range of flowers for sale.

4

Can you smell the creamy curry from that barge?

Here we are at the pop-up kitchens. Try not to shove. There's plenty to see!

This stall belongs to Mr Lee. He is no ordinary chef.
The rumour is that he cooks with a magic wok.
He says "Fry, little wok, fry!" and the wok fills
with noodles!

That's strange. Where is Mr Lee? This must be his magic wok. Am I the only hungry one?

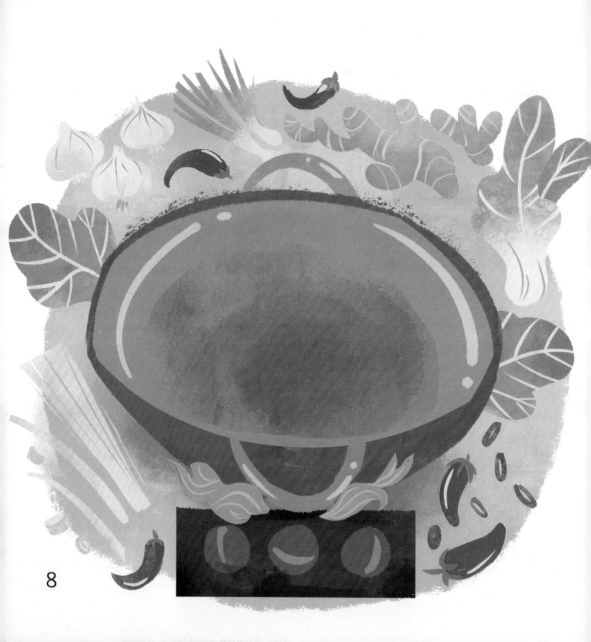

All I can think about is noodles!
Fry, little wok, fry!

sizzle

sizzle

9

These noodles are so tasty!

Fry, little wok, fry! Fry, little wok, fry! I've got oodles of noodles!

I wonder how Mr Lee makes the magic stop.
Please stop, wok! Wok, please stop! Stop wok, quick!

Help! There are oodles of noodles everywhere!
I wish Mr Lee was here!

14

Phew! Mr Lee! Your wok won't stop cooking!

16

I'm sorry Mr Lee. I'm to blame. I shouldn't have started cooking.

The market is covered in noodles. We'll have to stop the tour.

Unless ...

20

21

How to cook noodles

1. Heat oil in a pan.

2. Fry garlic and ginger.

3. Add noodles and stock.

4. Stir in vegetables.

5. Serve!

After reading

Letters and Sounds: Phase 5

Word count: 292

Focus phonemes: /ai/ a, eigh /ee/ e-e, e, y / igh/ y, i /ch/ tch /sh/ ch /j/ g, ge /l/ le /f/ ph /w/ wh /v/ ve /s/ se /z/ se

Common exception words: of, to, the, into, are, says, one, Mr

Curriculum links: Design and technology: Cooking and nutrition; Geography: Human and physical geography

National Curriculum learning objectives: Reading/word reading: apply phonic knowledge and skills as the route to decode words, read other words of more than one syllable that contain taught GPCs; Reading/comprehension: drawing on what they already know or on background information and vocabulary provided by the teacher

Developing fluency

- Your child may enjoy hearing you read the book.
- Take turns to read a page of text. Check that your child uses different voices for the characters and notices the exclamation marks in order to add emphasis to these sentences.

Phonic practice

- Turn to page 8. Challenge your child to find and read the words containing the /j/ sound. (*strange, magic*)
- Turn to page 5. Challenge your child to find and read the words containing the /ee/ sound. (*creamy, curry*) Can they identify the two different ways in which the /ee/ sound is written in **creamy**? (*ea, y*)
- Look through the book together, taking turns to find and read a word with the /j/ and /ee/ sounds.

Extending vocabulary

- Ask your child to suggest synonyms for each of the following:

  huge (e.g. *vast, massive*)   oodles (e.g. *lots, masses*)   strange (e.g. *odd, weird*)
- Ask your child to think of an antonym for each word too. (e.g. *tiny, limited; few, minimal; normal, predictable*)